# READY, SET, BUILD!

For my three little builders —
sketch a dream and go, go, go for it!

-M.F.

For Jenna

-J.

A TEMPLAR BOOK

First published in the UK in 2017 by Templar Publishing,
part of the Bonnier Publishing Group,
The Plaza, 535 King's Road, London, SW10 0SZ
www.templarco.co.uk
www.bonnierpublishing.com

First published in the U.S. in 2017 by little bee books,
part of the Bonnier Publishing Group

Text copyright © 2017 by Meg Fleming
Illustrations copyright © 2017 by Jarvis

1 3 5 7 9 10 8 6 4 2

ISBN 978-1-78370-809-3

Printed in China

# READY, SET, BUILD!

JARVIS                    MEG FLEMING

t

templar publishing

# Grab your hard hat,      tie your boots.

# Pack your lunch.

# Ready? Scoot!

# Sketch a dream. Draw a chart.

# Hatch the plan before you start.

# Move the rubble. Clear the space.
## Setting up is half the race.

Check the ground before you dig.
Make a hole that's deep and big.

# Keep your head up. Stay on track.

Use your legs and not your back.

Lift together, "1 – 2 – 3!"

# Break for lunch beneath a tree.

# Goggles on before you slice.
# Cut just once – but measure twice.

# Press the clutch when changing gears.
## If it's loud . . .

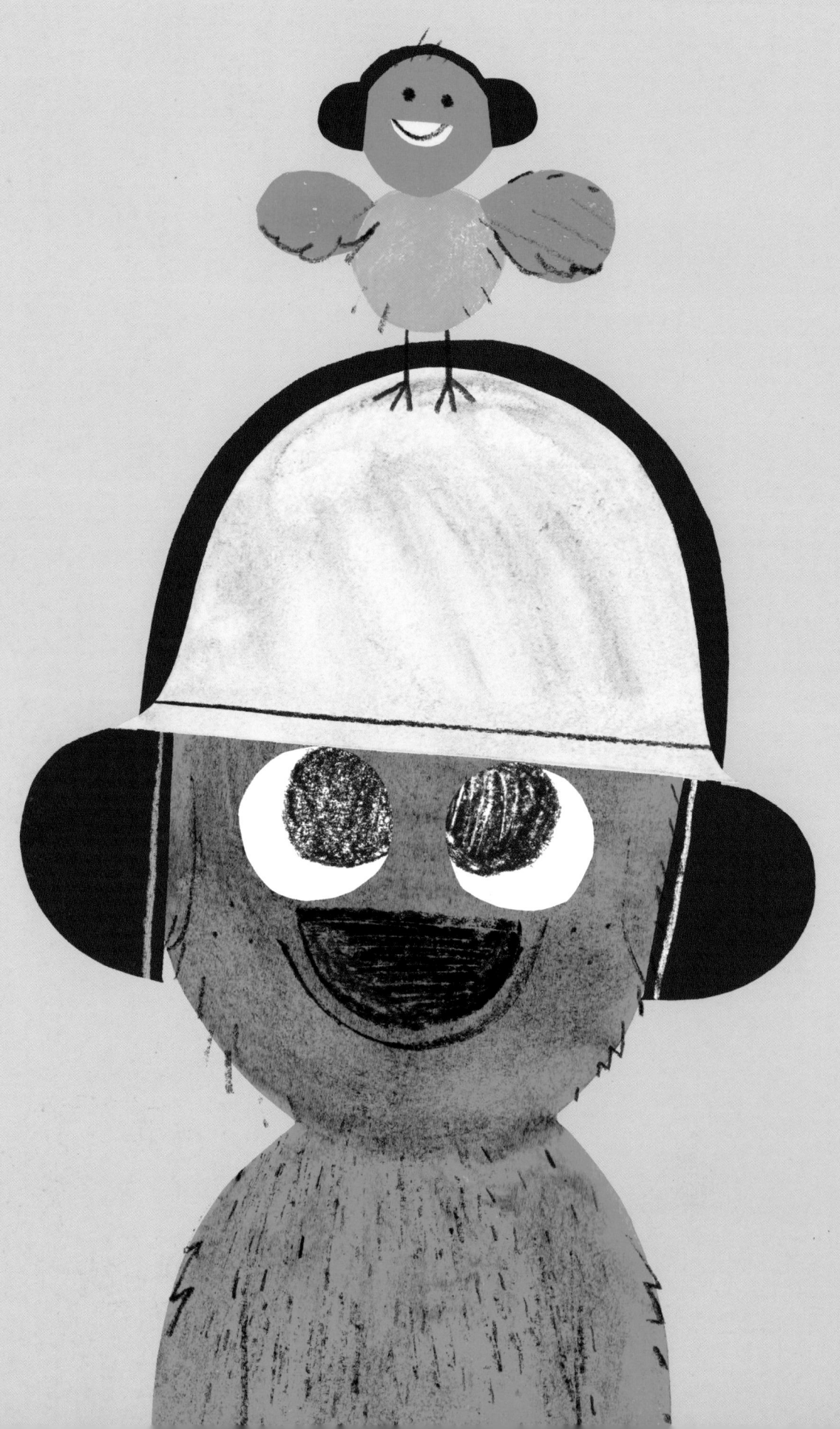

. . . plug your ears!

# Saw blades rasp and hammers crack!

# Cranes construct a tower stack.

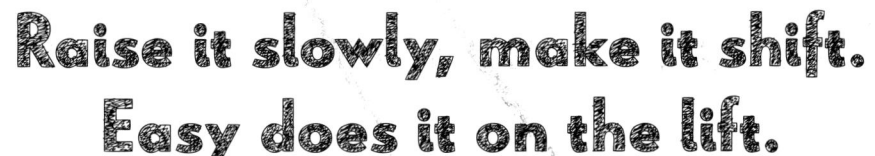

Raise it slowly, make it shift.
Easy does it on the lift.

# Windows in and roof tiles ready?

# Paint the walls and come down steady.

# Take a look. Enjoy your view.

# Sun goes home and so can you.

# Hang your hard hat. Job well done.

# Tomorrow's work . . .

. . . is twice the fun!